THE
SUMMER
OF THE
DANCING HORSE

Also by ETH CLIFFORD

Leah's Song
(original title: *The Man Who Sang in the Dark*)

Help! I'm a Prisoner in the Library

Just Tell Me When We're Dead

Scared Silly

THE
SUMMER
OF THE
DANCING HORSE

Eth Clifford

Inside illustrations by Mary Beth Owens

AN
APPLE
PAPERBACK

SCHOLASTIC INC.
New York Toronto London Auckland Sydney

ISBN 0-590-45400-5

12 11 10 9 8 7 6 5 4 3   2 3 4 5 6 7/9

Printed in the U.S.A.   28

First Scholastic printing, July 1992

For Ted Chichak,

with affection,

and

Jeannette Turgeon,

who swapped blueberry stories

with me

Contents

1

Bread in the Morning

"Bessie! Bessie Kobb! Rise and shine! Now!"

Her mother's voice from the kitchen below sounded the first warning.

Bessie smiled. She never needed that call, for the aroma of fresh-baked bread woke her every morning, threading its way into her dreams. She lay sprawled across her bed in the small attic room, her eyes half-closed, and tried to slip back into her dream world.

She had been flying, dipping and swirling low in a sky in which stars were fading reluctantly. Weightless, she floated toward the newly lit horizon. How sweet the dawn air was.

Bessie shook her head. It wasn't the dawn air that filled her room with a heady, rich fragrance. It was the bread Ma had been baking since before sunup — the bread and the pies and the muffins.

Bessie sat up to stare out the window. The woods seemed to march clear up to the back of the house, stopping a little way back politely, as if to give room to Ma's small vegetable garden. Elbow room, Ma called it.

Bessie took a deep breath. She loved the crisp pine air, sharp and tangy in the early morning, just as she loved the pine needles underfoot, spongy and yielding, when she walked through the woods. She had worn a path to where the lake lay quietly waiting, for sun and clouds and birds, and a brown-eyed, pigtailed, eight-year-old girl named Bessie Kobb.

"Things aren't people, Bessie," Ma told her time and again. "You can't give things people-feelings."

"How do we know they don't have feelings?" Bessie objected. "Don't you think the lake is glad when the water birds come back, and —"

"Now, Bessie," Ma interrupted firmly. "There's nothing wrong with imagining things, just so long as you keep your feet on the ground."

That was Ma, a down-to-earth person. Maybe, Bessie thought, tall, bony, serious-minded, hardworking people were all like Ma. But she could remember when Ma hadn't been grim all the time. Worry about Pa had turned her from a smiling woman to one who didn't remember how to laugh.

Pa was in a sanatorium because he had TB. Consumption, Ma called it. He was getting better, though.

Maybe, if he came home, Ma would be a smiling woman again.

Bessie sighed. Wasn't it funny how thoughts skipped around in your mind?

"Bessie. I won't call you again, hear?" This time Ma meant it. Bessie was always first to go to bed at night, and last to get up in the morning, but Ma would only stand for so much dawdling.

In a matter of minutes Bessie raced into the kitchen. Her twelve-year-old brother, Sam, frowned at her, his deep blue eyes darkening under his heavy black brows. He was impatient by nature, but especially so in the morning. While his sister had lazed in bed, Sam had been down to the cellar to bring up a scuttle of coal for the big black iron stove that took up so much space in the kitchen.

Long before sunup, while Bessie was still asleep, Ma had crumpled newspaper into the stove and piled it with wood chips. Then, she struck a long wooden match, threw it in, and waited for the flame to blaze. Only then did she cover it with coal.

It took a while for the stove to warm up. Ma whipped some eggs to a golden froth, then brushed them across the braided loaves waiting to go into the oven. It gave the breads a fine shine.

By the time Bessie came into the kitchen, the loaves

were all baked and sitting on cooling racks on the big
kitchen table.

"Will you get a move on?" Sam asked Bessie. "You
think I have all day?"

Ma tucked a few strands of brown hair back into the
scarf wrapped tightly around her head. Her eyes, the
same warm brown as Bessie's, were stern.

"There's time enough for Bessie to eat, Sam." Ma

was a firm believer that hot oatmeal, a thick slab of her potato bread drowning in butter, and milk would start the day right. "Now don't gulp your food," she cautioned, but Bessie gulped it anyway, for Sam was shuffling his feet restlessly.

If Sam became too impatient, he might not let her tag along after him the rest of the day. Then what would she do?

She could always go to the lake, of course, but Ma wouldn't let her take the canoe unless Sam was with her.

If it were a windy day, she could go to the cliff. There she would open Pa's big black umbrella, hang on to the handle, and fly. Ma didn't approve, but often she was too busy to know what Bessie was up to.

Bessie closed her eyes. She could feel the wind in her face, feel the umbrella tugging to sail into the breeze, feel that breathless moment when the ground fell away and she was free.

But it wasn't windy, so she announced, her mouth still full, "I'm ready."

Sam picked up two baskets piled high with loaves of bread, carefully wrapped in clean kitchen towels to keep them warm. Some of the breads were light and fluffy; others were round and dark and heavy, solid ryes and corn and potato loaves that satisfied hunger.

"You'll have to wait for Ben," Ma said. She glanced

at the clock and frowned. "He's late. I can't imagine what's keeping him."

"I know what's keeping him," Sam muttered. "He probably stopped to talk to a squirrel, or watch a weed grow, or something important like that."

Bessie studied her brother. Sam was so fast in everything he did. He had the quickest mind in the world probably, she thought. And Ben was slow — not stupid, just slow.

Ben would wait to watch the sun rise, or set, however long it might take. Sam just took it for granted that the sun would do what it was supposed to do. He couldn't take time to wait and see.

"Mini isn't here, either," Bessie reminded her mother.

Mini was a dog who belonged to Doc Hawkins, a vet who lived a couple of miles down the road. It didn't bother Doc Hawkins that Mini wasn't a collie, or an Irish setter, or a terrier, or anything you could put a name to. She was just a mixture no one had ever figured out for sure.

"That's okay," Doc always said. "Mini suits me, and I suit her. And that's good enough for both of us." He'd named her Mini because she was so tiny as a puppy. She'd grown up big and shaggy, but the name stuck.

Mini and Ben came from different directions, but

always arrived at the same time. Ben came to help deliver the bread; Mini came out of greed. Ma always set aside a soup bone for her.

Ma looked at the clock again and sighed. "You'd better go along, Sam."

She handed a basket to Bessie. It, too, was lined with towels, but held only muffins. Bessie claimed she could carry a heavier load if Ma would let her. But Ma just shook her head. It was a long, slow, sometimes hot walk even in the early June morning sun to Rosie Dugal's country store.

Ma held the kitchen door open for them.

"Ben!" Bessie said.

A slender boy sat cross-legged on the steps. He turned and glanced up at them, his large, gray eyes troubled.

"Didn't you know we were waiting for you? Why on earth didn't you come in?" Mrs. Kobb asked.

"Mini isn't here." Ben's words came out spaced apart, as if he had to remember how to put the words together.

"So what?" Sam shifted the baskets, which seemed to grow heavier the longer he held them. "Maybe she decided to stay home with her puppies."

"Maybe she's already weaned them," Ma said. "Those puppies are a month old now."

"That wouldn't stop Mini. She'd never miss coming

for her bone." Bessie agreed with Ben. Mini should have been here long ago.

Sam squatted down beside Ben.

"Listen. We have to deliver the bread. So let's do that first. Then Bessie and I will help you look for Mini, okay?"

Bessie stared at Ben. He was thirteen years old, but Sam always talked to him as if he were a small child.

Ben didn't mind. He smiled.

"I know," he said. "Bread. Bread in the morning."

2

Tunes in the Sunlight

"I just love mornings," Bessie announced, as she followed her brother and Ben to the road. Bessie was a talker. If there was no one around to listen, Bessie often spoke her thoughts aloud. What was the use of having a voice if you never used it? she often asked Sam. Ma said people shouldn't talk unless they had something important to say. But how could you tell what was important until you said it out loud and heard what it sounded like?

"There was a mockingbird outside my window this morning," Bessie went on. "I just wish I could whistle like that bird." She pursed her lips. She could whistle some, but nothing that ever came out as a real tune.

Sam shrugged. "Why? It's only a bird that imitates every other birdcall."

"Is that bad? Is it wrong?" Ben was always eager to learn, though he had a hard time remembering what people told him.

"I don't want to imitate anybody, that's what's wrong. I just want to be me, Sam Kobb. That's good enough for me." Sam walked more quickly, pulling ahead of the other two.

As she and Ben hurried to catch up with him, Bessie thought about her brother. Sam had a strong, independent mind, Ma said. He knew from the time he was six exactly what he wanted to do when he was grown. He was going to build bridges — bigger bridges, better bridges — all around the world.

Sam had sturdy, broad hands with long, nimble fingers. He was tall for his age, too, with a fine-muscled body. And he had the distant gaze in his eyes that Ma called his "future" look, as if he could see into the years to come and liked what he saw.

I'm eight, Bessie pondered, and I don't even know yet what I want to be when I'm big.

Ma didn't think that was a problem. "Just you be a child first," she said. "You'll be grown up a long, long time."

Ben had caught up with Sam easily, but Bessie lagged behind. She watched as the two boys quickened their steps, to see which one could take longer strides.

What would Ben be when he was grown? He couldn't read very well; his speech was slow. His father was a surly man, with gray eyes hard as marbles and a thin, tight mouth. He was always rough with Ben. Mr. Tobin took Ben on hunting and fishing trips even though he knew his son hated it. Ben shuddered away from the killing of animals, but Mr. Tobin wouldn't put up with that. Sometimes Ben hid in Sam's room, but there was no escape. Mr. Tobin always came after him.

"I'll make a man of that boy," he told Ma, hitting a willow switch against his leg. "You mollycoddle those kids of yours. That's what comes of no man around the house."

"You're mean spirited and cruel," Ma Kobb said. "If anyone needs to be switched, it's you. Some day that boy will turn on you, mark my words."

Mr. Tobin laughed. "I'd sure enough like to see him try."

"That man," Ma sputtered when he left with Ben. "That terrible man. He ain't worth salt for peanuts."

Bessie didn't realize how far she had fallen behind the boys while she was busy thinking. Now she yelled, "Hey! Wait for me, will you?"

But Ben had already stopped walking. "Oh! I forgot." He placed his baskets carefully on the road, then dug into his pocket. As Bessie came close, he pulled out a large maple leaf, which was folded around several mushrooms he had picked in the woods. Ben had tried to teach Sam and Bessie about mushrooms, but

Sam wasn't interested and Bessie couldn't remember. She did like the names of some Ben had warned her not to pick. One was the Fly, the other the Destroying Angel. That made her shiver. The mushrooms that Ben had wrapped in the maple leaf were a delicate beige and white. Meadow mushrooms, Ben called them.

"Okay. We've seen the mushrooms. Now can we get going?"

Ben was apologetic but firm. "No, Sam. I have to give these to Ma Kobb, to make soup."

Ma made soup for lunch every day, and never told them what kind it would be. Bessie thought of them as Ma's mystery soups, but Ma called them stick-to-your-ribs soups. Lunch was always better than supper, which might be just mashed potatoes and creamed corn.

"Eat light. Sleep tight," Ma said, but she didn't look too happy saying it.

Sam, watching Ben run back, muttered, "Dumb kid."

"Is he dumb because he forgets? Mr. Tobin says Ben is the dumbest kid in the whole world."

"He's a fine one to talk," Sam snapped. "He's a real sour apple, that one."

Bessie persisted in her questions, even though Sam was annoyed. "How come Ben isn't smart, Sam?

You're smart. You do arithmetic in your head faster than I can write the numbers down. And I can read better than Ben. I even have to read to him sometimes."

"There's all kinds of smart, Bessie. You ever watch Ben's eyes? Sometimes I think Ben can say more with his eyes than we can say with words."

Bessie nodded. "And he knows the woods better than you —"

"And he can run faster than a jack rabbit," Sam interrupted. "See?" He pointed down the road. "He runs so fast he can meet himself coming back."

Breathless but content, Ben swung by, scooped up the baskets of pies, and raced on.

"Beat you," he called back, smiling.

"You go on," Bessie urged her brother. "I'll catch up."

As Bessie plodded along far behind, she tilted her head and listened intently. Rosie Dugal's country store wasn't too far off, and right about now she should be hearing music.

There! It was faint, but her hearing was keen.

By the time she reached Rosie's, Sam and Ben were coming out of the store empty-handed. Ben snatched Bessie's basket, ran into the store and out again. His gray eyes were shining with expectation.

Now the music was louder. Soon Doc Hawkins came

into view, a husky man, broad in the shoulders, a black cloth cap on his head, and a harmonica almost invisible cupped in his heavy hands. He had lost his only son in the Great War back in 1918, five years ago. He had stopped playing for a while; now, though, the sounds he made were sprightly. His tunes made even the sunlight appear brighter.

Doc Hawkins was followed by a creamy-gold palomino horse. Her whitish mane was a ripple of sunbeams. She swayed and pranced, swished her golden tail, and dipped her head while Doc Hawkins' merry notes filled the morning air.

Bessie began to dance, too, throwing her arms out, spinning and leaping.

Dancing horse and dancing girl came to a stop in front of the store. Rosie came out, her hands on her wide hips, her fat face crinkled in a broad grin, and shouted a welcome. Grover Abbott, who owned the farm next to Doc Hawkins', followed, clapping his hands. His son Ned was there, too. He had gone off to war with Doc Hawkins' son. He had come back limping and pale and grim, and the only time he ever nearly smiled anymore was at the sight of the dancing horse and girl. Other regulars piled out as well; it was too early in the morning for most of the summer people.

Finally the music ceased. Doc Hawkins swept his

hat from his head and bowed. The horse and child bowed as well.

"We've come for our bread and muffins and pie," Doc Hawkins announced.

"Come and get it, fresh from the oven," Rosie said.

"Just keep an eye on Pegasus for me, will you, Sam?"

Ben thought it was a hard name for a horse, even though Doc Hawkins had explained it.

"She comes so close to flying without wings when she dances, I thought naming her for a flying horse was a good idea."

Bessie agreed. She knew how it felt to want to fly.

She and Sam and Ben stroked Pegasus, but it was Ben who whispered in the horse's ear as Pegasus in turn bent her head and began to nuzzle him gently.

3

The Summer Man

Bessie followed Doc Hawkins into the store eagerly. Even though the store and everything in it was familiar, Bessie still found it a place of magic.

She paid no attention to the long shelves behind the counter, for all the usual things were there — the cans of condensed milk stacked next to the laundry soap, bolts of bright-colored cloth jostling the items Rosie called notions, and everything else the farm women came to buy. In front of the counter, barrels held soda crackers and flour and sugar.

Bessie skirted around these, and half glanced at the dressmaker's dummy that stood beside them. Rosie changed the dress on the dummy every three months or so. The dummy wore the same dress that Bessie had last seen, so she passed it by quickly, her eye on a long glass case. Inside the case, on two shining glass shelves, was an assortment of candies that made Bessie lick her lips.

"Mmmmm," she said, as she pressed her nose hard against the glass. She sighed. There they all were — the chick feed, which was really candy corn; the jawbreakers, which hadn't ever broken anyone's jaw, so far as Bessie knew; the foxy grandpas. Bessie sighed again. They were pink-and-white marshmallows that looked like little old men. And, of course, the black licorice whips and the red licorice whips. Yes, there it all was, and more, an untouchable feast.

Ma saw no reason to spend pennies on store-bought when she made perfectly good peanut brittle and fudge at home.

Ma just didn't understand. It was like saying the dresses Ma made for her were just as good, and better, than store-bought ones.

Looking at the candy in Rosie's store was like turning the pages in the Sears, Roebuck catalogue, something to dream about.

Bessie closed her eyes and imagined Rosie sliding back the door to the case, reaching in, smiling at Bessie, and then. . . . It had never happened, but wouldn't it be wonderful if just once . . .

A man's demanding voice made Bessie turn around. She didn't know his name, but she recognized him. The summer man, Bessie told herself. He belonged with those other people who flocked to the lake each year like migrating birds. Bessie sometimes watched

the summer boys and girls from the branch of a tree. She wondered if they would be friendly if she spoke to them, but she was too shy to approach them. Ma was delighted when the summer people came, for they swarmed to Rosie's to buy Ma's home-baked goods.

The man was taller than Doc Hawkins. The rimless glasses he pinched on his thin nose made his dark eyes seem large and angry. His teeth were fine and even and remarkably white under his bushy black mustache. Rosie said he was a "swell," which she insisted was the name for the summer men who wore white trousers, double-breasted blue jackets with shining brass buttons, and fancy straw hats.

His appearance fascinated Bessie. She'd never seen Pa in anything but dungarees. The summer man was like a cypress tree, all swept upward, Bessie thought. Pa was a willow, drooping, a gentle whisper. But Doc Hawkins was an oak, strong, solid, not one to bend to the will of the wind.

It was a good thing Ma couldn't see Bessie's thoughts. She'd worry that Bessie was reading too many fanciful books.

"You can't always be dreaming," Ma would say.

Bessie snapped to attention. The summer man was saying, "Have you thought about my offer for Pegasus?"

Doc Hawkins said, not impatiently, though he told the summer man the same thing every morning, "She's not for sale."

"But I'll pay whatever you ask." The summer man said that every morning, too.

Doc Hawkins simply shook his head.

Bessie had once asked her brother why the summer man wanted Pegasus so much.

Sam had shrugged. "When he saw Pegasus dance, he wanted to ride her, and Doc Hawkins wouldn't let him."

"But nobody ever rides her," Bessie pointed out.

"Doc's son, Vergil, did. And sometimes Doc does. Doc explained that once, but that only made the summer man dig in his heels. Ma says some people are bound and determined to have their way, no matter what."

"I don't want him to have Pegasus." Bessie was angry. "I don't want him ever to have Pegasus."

"Well, he won't."

Bessie was relieved, until her brother added, "Not unless he wears Doc down."

Now Bessie watched the two men warily. The summer man's face reddened; he rubbed his mustache hard with his fist. Then, suddenly, he smiled. "Of course," he said, softly, as if speaking to himself. "You're not a man to be persuaded by words. I should have thought of that before."

He picked up the bread and muffins he had come for and headed for the door. There he turned and said over his shoulder, "I'll have Pegasus, wait and see."

Bessie gave Doc Hawkins a worried look. He smiled

at her and at Rosie, whose laugh filled the room like the bray of a donkey.

"He's a high-muck-a-muck, that one. Used to having his own way, he is. Say, listen," she said, winking at Doc Hawkins, "when it comes to stubborn, I'll put my money on you."

Doc Hawkins didn't answer, just picked up his bread and pie and muffins, and started to leave. At that moment, Sam came in, frowning.

"Ben and I have been waiting for you, Bessie. Will you get a move on?"

"Mini!" Bessie clapped her hand to her mouth. "I forgot."

Doc Hawkins swiveled his head to stare at her.

"What about Mini?"

"She never came to the house this morning," Sam explained. "Ben is real worried."

"That fool dog." Doc Hawkins wasn't upset at all. "Forever off chasing something. She'll show up. Just give her time."

He went out, letting the screen door bang shut behind him. Sam and Bessie could hear him talking to Ben, and Ben's slow voice. In a moment, Ben joined them in the store.

"Doc says Mini's okay. But I want to look for her anyway." Ben pushed the words out even more slowly than usual. It happened whenever he was deeply distressed.

But Sam paid no attention. He had noticed something on one of the shelves behind the counter.

"Is that what I think it is?" he asked in a whisper.

Rosie didn't bother to look. She just jerked her thumb over her shoulder. She knew exactly what had caught Sam's eye. Rosie had been waiting to see how long it would take Sam to discover it.

"It sure is," she said.

"I want it," Sam said.

Bessie caught her breath. He sounded just like the summer man then. Was this how it began, when you were still a kid?

Ben tugged at Sam's arm. "You promised," he pleaded.

Sam shook him off impatiently.

"I've got to have that Erector Set," he told Rosie. "I've just got to."

"Sure." Rosie shrugged. "Just like somebody is going to want these."

She placed a small box on the counter. Bessie edged closer to see what it held, then gasped. Not even in the Sears, Roebuck catalogue had she ever seen anything so beautiful. Displayed on tissue paper, a pair of white satin gloves gleamed in a slanting ray of sunshine. Delicate lace and tiny pink pearls trimmed the cuffs.

"Oh, Rosie." Bessie sighed, and the longing in her voice caught Sam's attention. He turned momentarily away from the Erector Set.

"Where did they come from?" Sam asked.

"One of the summer ladies. Her little girl wore these to a wedding. Wore them only once. Now she's outgrown them. The mother's asking a dollar twenty-five."

"For *gloves?*" Sam asked, incredulously. "One dollar and twenty-five cents, for *gloves?*"

When he saw how his sister yearned toward them, reaching out a tentative hand, wanting to touch that incredible fabric, he told her gently, "Bessie, even if we had money to spare, Ma would never let you have them. They're not *practical.*"

Bessie nodded. If Ma disapproved of store-bought candy, she'd be shocked at the notion of fancy gloves. She could almost hear Ma say, "But when would you *wear* them?"

Nonetheless, Bessie made up her mind. Someday she'd have it all — the candy and the gloves. She didn't know how just yet. But she could be as stubborn as Sam when he wanted something. And as determined as Ma. Especially like Ma.

Ben had been standing by silently, puzzled but waiting. Now he could wait no longer.

"Sam," he begged. "Can we go now? Please. We've got to find Mini."

4

The Blueberry Plan

Disregarding Ben, Sam moved back to study the Erector Set. He could see a picture of a soaring bridge on the cover of the box. On impulse, he turned and lifted Bessie. "See the bridge on the box, Bessie? I could build that, and more."

"That's what Pa promised to get you," she told him as he put her down again. "An Erector Set. I remember."

"That was before." Sam's voice was somber. He didn't say the words, but Bessie knew what he meant. That was before Pa got sick and went away.

"Where did you get it, Rosie?" Bessie wanted to know. Rosie had never had toys in the store.

"One of the summer kids left it here. Said I could sell it for twelve dollars."

Bessie stared from Sam to Rosie to the Erector Set. Twelve dollars! That might as well be all the money in the world. As if Sam's heart was in her body, she could feel its heavy weight sinking down, clear down to her bare feet.

Ben didn't understand what was going on, Bessie could see that. How could Sam explain why it was so important?

She reached out to stop Ben's hand from tugging Sam's arm, but she was too late. Ben pulled hard. "We have to look for Mini. You promised."

"Shhh." Sam's voice was sharp. "Not now. Can't you see I'm thinking?"

Ben drew back, his eyes wide with hurt. "But you *promised,*" he insisted, bewildered.

Sam, however, was lost in his dream, his eyes fixed on the Erector Set. He wasn't aware that Ben went silently from the store. But Bessie noticed.

"Sam, listen. Ben just —"

Her brother waved his hand at her, as if brushing away a bothersome fly. "Be quiet." He turned to Rosie. "I have to have that set, Rosie You know how much I want it."

Rosie put her hands on her hips. She was a big woman, with plump cheeks stained a permanent red. Her short, fair hair grew like a puffball around her head. She wore colors so bright they dazzled the eye. This morning her dress was a strong green on which huge, impossible flowers ran wild. She looked, Bessie thought, as though she had rolled over and over in a blooming meadow and come away with part of the meadow still wrapped around her.

"Wanting isn't getting, is it?" Rosie asked.

"You could trust him for the money," Bessie said hopefully.

Rosie shook her head and pointed to a sign nailed to one of the shelves. TRUST IS BUST it said in overlarge letters. She reached down behind the counter and pulled out a cigar box.

"I can't put trust in here." She tapped the box vigorously. "Cash. Give it to me in dollars, or give it to me in pennies." She rattled the box in the air. "You hear that? Cash! I like your Ma. I pay her cash. I like you kids, but business is business, and I'm not in it for my health."

She put the cigar box away with a loud thump, then waited to see what Sam would say.

"Wait a minute. I have an idea," Sam began.

Rosie nodded. "Sure you do. I could see your brain working from here."

Bessie stared at her brother. How did Rosie do that? She couldn't see Sam's brain working at all.

"I could earn it," Sam suggested. "I could help you in the store, sweep out, put stuff away on the shelves. I could —"

"Could me no coulds," Rosie interrupted. She narrowed her pale blue eyes. Rosie claimed a body

28

couldn't think with her eyes wide open.

"All right," she told Sam finally. "I don't need you in the store. But pick me some blueberries. The summer people like fresh-picked berries. I'll pay you five cents a pail. Now that's for nice ripe *blue* blueberries. No little green ones. No twigs. No leaves. Yes or no?"

"Yes," Sam agreed promptly. "But you have to supply the pails."

"Mind the store. I'll fetch some pails from the back."

While she was gone, Sam turned to his sister. "You have to help me. And Ben has to help, too. I have my chores and all, but I figure if we pick fast, we can make two dollars a week. That way I could get the set in six weeks. Is that okay with you, Ben?" Sam blinked. "Where's Ben? Where did he go?"

"Don't you remember? We were supposed to help him find Mini. He was almost crying when he went out."

Sam was upset. "He should have waited."

As soon as Rosie returned with the pails — two for Sam and two for Bessie — Sam ran for the door. Over his shoulder, he called, "You put that set away for me, Rosie, hear?"

He didn't wait for Rosie's nod.

"Are we going to pick blueberries now?" Bessie yelled as she chased after her brother.

"Don't you know anything?" he shouted back impatiently. "We have to find Ben first. I promised him we'd look for Mini."

"But we don't know where Ben went," Bessie wailed.

"Ben probably figured Mini went to her favorite hunting place in the woods. Anyway, that's a place to start with."

Now that a decision had been made, Bessie didn't mind that Sam shot on ahead. She knew the area as well as he did. As she walked along, she could hear her brother calling, "Ben! Ben!"

The call grew fainter as Sam moved out of sight. For a while the comforting silence enfolded her. Then she became aware of small, skittering sounds, and a titter of choked laughter she immediately recognized.

She whirled around. Though she saw no one, she shouted angrily, "I know you're there, Luke Keefer. And you, too, Purley."

Two boys emerged from behind one of the bushes that dotted the roadside. Luke Keefer was ten months older than his eleven-year-old brother Purley, but they might almost have been twins. Both were heavy-set, with sandy hair cut so short it was almost invisible. Both had brown eyes, mean and cunning. Both wore ragged dungarees shorn at the knees, and no shirts.

"Well, look what we got here, Purley," Luke said in

a high-pitched, mincing voice. "The girl who dances with horses. Want to dance for us, Bessie?"

Luke pitched a small hailstorm of pebbles around Bessie's feet. Purley immediately followed suit.

Bessie's face paled as the pebbles stung her ankles. Then she leaned down, scooped up some of the pebbles, and let fly. Her aim was remarkably true. She caught Purley on the forehead, and Luke on his right cheek.

"Hey! You could have put my eye out," Purley yelled. He brought his hand down from his forehead and stared at it. "Look! I'm bleeding."

"You pester me anymore and I'll knock your brains out, if you have any." Then Bessie pretended to hear her brother's voice. "I'm here, Sam. Over here."

The Keefer brothers looked about apprehensively. They often tormented Ben, and when they thought it was safe, harried Bessie. But not when Sam was around, for he was ferocious in a fight. He would protect Bessie and Ben even if it meant taking on both brothers at the same time.

They began to move off, scuffing at the road with their bare feet, shouting back over their shoulders.

Messy Bessie,
Her Ma bakes bread,
'Cause Bessie has a Pa
Who is halfway dead.

Bessie clenched her hands into knuckle-whitened fists. It wasn't true. Pa wasn't halfway dead. He had TB, and people died of it, but not her Pa. He hadn't died in the war. And he wouldn't die now. He was a fighting man. He'd told her and Sam, "Don't you give up on me now. I'm not going anywhere till I've seen you kids strong and grown. You have my word on it."

And Pa had smiled, a bright smile that warmed them, though he wouldn't permit them to come close.

Bessie turned away from the Keefer boys to continue following Sam. As she walked on, she was so lost in thought that she almost stumbled over her brother, who was kneeling on the ground, worrying his lower lip with his fingers as he stared downward.

When he heard her footsteps, he looked up. Then he held a warning hand in the air.

Bessie dropped to her knees, to stare wide-eyed at a fox lying cold and still on the ground. "Is it dead?" Her voice was hushed. When Sam nodded, she reached out to stroke the animal's fur. Its beautiful red coat shone where sunbeams flickered through the trees. "You think someone killed her?" Bessie's thoughts flashed to Mr. Tobin. He hated foxes, said they were always after his chickens.

"I don't know, Bessie. It doesn't look as though she's been shot. I don't want to touch her to find out." Sam pulled his sister up. "Come on. Let's go."

But Bessie turned her head. "Wait!"

"Now what?" Bessie had a keen ear, but Sam couldn't hear a sound. "Is it Ben?"

"Shhh. There it is. It's coming from over there." Bessie pointed to a hollow log. "I think an animal is hurt."

"I'll take a look. You wait here." Bessie ignored the command and followed Sam. He peered inside, whistled, and put his hand gingerly in the log. "A cub. It sure is scrawny. Wait. There's another one. They look as if they haven't had food for quite a while. I guess that was the mother we found."

Sam started to put the cubs back in the log. "We'd better leave them where we found them. The father fox might be somewhere around."

"What difference would that make?"

"He'll take care of them. Maybe he's off hunting for food."

"It doesn't look like he's been taking care of them at all. The poor little babies. They'll die. We have to take them with us."

Bessie picked up a cub and stared at Sam defiantly.

"Okay. We'll take them to Doc Hawkins. He'll know what to do. Give them here. I'll carry them."

Bessie said urgently, "Sam! That's Ben! He's crying!"

Sam tumbled the cubs into the blueberry pails, one

in each, then took off in the direction of the sound.

Bessie followed as quickly as she could, afraid of what lay ahead, as Ben's sobs grew louder and more anguished.

5

A Pailful of Foxes

Bessie was shocked when she reached the two boys. Mini was caught in an animal trap, its ugly pointed edges stabbing her thigh. Sam was on his knees, examining the trap thoughtfully. Ben gazed at Sam with hope; he always felt the other boy could handle any situation. Bessie knew that; mostly, she agreed her brother was the most dependable boy around.

"What happened?" Bessie shook her head, angry at herself for asking when it was clear enough what had happened. Mini had fallen into the trap while she was sniffing around, and the blood on Ben's hands must have come from Mini's leg as Ben tried to free her.

Not all of it, Bessie suddenly realized.

"Sam," she said. "Ben's hurt. He's bleeding."

"I know. He cut his hands on the trap." Sam sounded indifferent, but Bessie understood. Sam tried to solve problems one at a time. Ben could wait; Mini couldn't.

"What are we going to do?" Bessie was impatient. Why was it taking Sam so long to make up his mind to do something? "Maybe I better go get somebody."

Sam held his hand up. "Hold your horses, will you? The first thing we've got to do is get Mini out, *now*." He tapped the trap. "Look. See how old and rusty it is? A couple of pieces are broken off right here. And the teeth haven't snapped closed all the way. We ought to be able to pry them open."

Bessie leaned in closer.

Sam sighed. "Will you put your pails down? You're going to need both hands to help."

Bessie dropped her pails next to those holding the cubs, peered in at them, then cried in alarm, "Sam. One of them is moving around."

"They're not going anywhere. They're too frightened. Now listen, Bessie. I want you and Ben to pull together on the other side of the trap when I say 'go.' I'll pull from this side."

Ben's face brightened. "You think we can get it open?"

Sam was cautious. You had to be careful when you made a promise to Ben. He expected you to keep your word. "I don't know, Ben. But we can try."

Bessie grasped the trap, gritting her teeth when the rusty metal scraped her hands. Ben disregarded the blood on his hands as he, too, seized the trap.

36

On the other side, Sam asked, "Ready?" When they nodded, he gripped the trap and yelled, "GO!"

All three tugged, straining to widen the gap. Mini watched with pain-filled eyes, and whimpered. Bessie winced as a long scratch on her palm began to throb and bleed.

"That's enough," Sam ordered. "Ben and I can do this by ourselves. You go sit down."

"No." Her mouth set in a stubborn line, Bessie wrapped her hands around the trap again.

Once again, Sam asked, "Ready?"

"Go!" Bessie shouted.

"It moved," Ben said.

Sam shook his head. "Not enough. Let's rest a minute and try again."

"I don't want to rest." Ben seized the trap in such a tight grip his knuckles jutted out.

Sam rubbed his hands hard down the side of his pants to remove tiny particles of rust from his palms.

"Ready," Ben said.

"Go." Sam closed his eyes and set his jaw.

The trap creaked. Slowly, very slowly, the teeth of the trap pulled away. There was a small but visible gap now.

Mini whined, softly, and tried to get out.

Sam reached out a comforting hand. "Not yet, Mini. Not yet."

He nodded at the others.

"NOW!"

Ben yanked so hard he fell over backward, hitting his head. He sat up, slightly dazed, then reached in to free Mini. The jagged metal teeth tore at her as he tugged, and Mini whimpered.

Sam reached in on the other side of the trap and pushed Mini upward.

"Don't stop," he told Ben. "I know we're hurting her, but we can't stop now."

"You've got her," Bessie cried.

Ben hugged Mini, then put her down gently. The dog struggled to stand, but sank down at once. She licked Ben's hand as he reached out to stroke her. "She's hurt real bad. She's going to die, isn't she?"

"No, she isn't." Bessie was furious. "Don't you say things like that, Ben Tobin."

She remembered the still body of the mother fox. She'd been sorry when she saw her stretched out lifeless on the ground, and she was sorry now. But this was Mini, their Mini. She couldn't die. They wouldn't let her.

Just the same, she turned anxiously to her brother. "Is her leg broken? Did she bleed too much, Sam?"

"I can't tell, Bessie. But we can help her a little. You and Ben find me some large wet leaves. You'll find damp ones in the shade. There should still be some covered with dew."

When Bessie and Ben came back with the leaves, they found that Sam had used his pocket knife to cut some long vines.

"You going to make a poultice?" Bessie asked.

Sam didn't bother to answer, just took the leaves and placed them gently on Mini's injury. He then tied them in place with the vines, knotting them tightly to keep the leaves in place.

"That feels good, doesn't it, Mini?" Bessie had a

feeling Mini understood, for the dog had turned her head and gazed up at Bessie with love.

Sam stood up, brushing his hands together. "We've got to get her to Doc Hawkins. Help me lift her."

"I want to carry her," Ben said. He glared down at the broken pieces of metal on the ground, suddenly kicking them out of the way.

"Pa and his traps," he cried.

"Wait a minute, Ben," Sam objected. "You don't know that. A trap this old, anybody could have set it."

But Ben's face had a cold, hard look, and his eyes remembered all his past hurts.

"Your pa likes dogs," Bessie reminded Ben. "He's never laid a hand on Buddy Boy. You know that. He thinks the world of that dog of his."

She was surprised to hear herself defending Mr. Tobin, but it was true, she thought. All his affection seemed to center on Buddy Boy. He would hit Ben, and often for no good reason, but he had never harmed Buddy Boy.

"Never mind all that," Sam put in impatiently. "You can start out with Mini, but when you get tired, I'll take over. Understood?"

Ben nodded. He kneeled down and waited for Sam to drape Mini around his shoulders. Sam then picked up the two pails in which the fox cubs nestled. Sam walked beside Ben, keeping watch, ready to take over

if he needed to. Bessie swung her empty pails back
and forth as she followed behind them.

Neither Sam nor Ben noticed that one of the fox
cubs, more daring than the other, was peering out
over the edge of a pail. Bessie smiled, then looked
down into her own empty containers.

We came to pick blueberries, she thought, and got
fox cubs instead.

6

Treasures in the Creek

"I'm tired," Bessie complained. "We've been walking for hours." The road seemed so much longer going back — longer, dustier, hotter.

Sam turned to study his sister thoughtfully. "We've only covered a little more than a mile. That's not even halfway back to Doc's place."

"I don't care. I'm tired. And thirsty, too."

"Okay. I know a good place for us to stop."

"No," Ben objected. "No stopping." But he shifted Mini slightly and hunched his shoulders forward.

"You're even more tired than I am," Bessie challenged him. "And maybe Mini needs a rest from her bumpy ride, too."

"Bessie's right, Ben. We've just got to rest a couple of minutes. It won't make that much difference to Mini, will it, you poor old thing?"

Sam could sure be a loving person, Bessie thought. He never could stand to see anyone suffer, not Pa, not

Ben, not anybody. He had once given Luke Keefer a black eye for tormenting a cat, and wouldn't apologize, though Mrs. Keefer demanded Sam say he was sorry.

Though Ben was tired, he insisted they go on. But when Sam said firmly, "We have to rest," Ben reluctantly agreed. Sam led them a short way off the road along a narrow path.

"We're going to Felton's Creek. I forgot it was so close." Bessie was delighted. She never came here anymore, for it was too far from home. It hadn't seemed far when she was with Pa, but then he had often carried her part of the way. She was too big to be carried now, and Pa . . . Bessie didn't want to think about how thin and spindly Pa had looked when he left for the sanatorium.

Ma had once told Bessie that she and Pa used to picnic along Felton's Creek when they were courting. "We don't know any Feltons, Ma, do we?" Bessie had asked. Mrs. Kobb shook her head. No one knew what had happened to the Felton family, but the name remained to remind everyone that Feltons had owned this land long ago.

Mostly, the creek took its time meandering through the woods, lilting now and then when it curled around rocks that jutted up from the creek bed. But Bessie had seen it after a summer storm, when the creek rushed by like a small, busy river, hurrying to some distant, imagined sea.

When they reached the creek, Ben sank down with a sigh. Sam eased Mini from Ben's shoulders and laid her gently on the ground. First he carefully removed the bandage of leaves and vines. Then he took a large handkerchief from his pocket, dipped it in the cool water, then sponged Mini's wound gently. She looked up at him with grateful eyes, and tried to wag her tail.

Ben stared at her, unsmiling, his face set. "I hate my Pa," he said. "I'll never go hunting with him again."

Bessie started to speak, but Sam motioned for her to follow him to the creek.

"There's no use talking to him when he's like this," he told his sister. He let the water run over his bruised palms, then examined them closely. The trap had torn his skin. Carrying the foxes in the pails had rubbed angry red streaks in the sore spots.

Bessie, meanwhile, having washed her face and hands, had plunged her feet into the creek. "Aaaah! That feels so good!"

Sam kneeled on the low bank, swished the water back and forth, then leaned over and lapped at the water. In a moment, Bessie was beside him, cupping water in her hands and drinking it.

"What about Ben? He looks too tired to move."

"I'll bring him water in a pail. Enough for Mini and the cubs, too. And when we leave, I'll carry Mini."

From the way Sam spoke, Bessie knew he would not allow Ben to argue with him. When Ben joined her, she knew the matter was settled.

"From the way you looked, I didn't think you could make it to the creek."

"I have blood on my hands," Ben said, his voice somber, then looked away as the water turned pink as he washed.

Bessie didn't mind the sight of blood, but she knew it made Ben sick. To distract him, she asked, "You think anyone ever found gold in this creek?"

She waded into the creek to peer down at the bottom.

For the first time that day, Ben smiled, his gray eyes lightening with fun. "I'll find gold for you." Ben joined her in the creek. "Look." He pointed. "Better than gold." He reached down where the water ran shallow against the low bank. He scooped something up, then showed his treasure to Bessie.

"Skipping stones! Oh, Ben, they're beautiful." Bessie examined them closely. Two were a shade of quiet gray, one had a bluish tinge, three were white touched with a faint pink.

Bessie ran her fingers over them, enjoying the feel of the flat, smooth, round stones. Bessie was better

45

than most at sending stones skimming across the lake at home. She could create a stream of ripples in widening circles. Sam was good, too, but Ben could beat both of them.

Good skipping stones were hard to find. Wasn't it just like Ben to discover them, Bessie thought. She was glad, for now his black mood had lifted completely.

"I have a nice deep pocket, Bessie. You want me to hold the stones for you?"

Bessie nodded. Ben held the pocket open, and smiled as Bessie dropped the treasured stones in, one at a time.

"Now don't you forget to give them back to me when we get home," Bessie ordered. "They're probably the best stones I ever will have. I'll make the biggest, widest, best ripples on that lake anybody ever saw. You wait and see, Ben."

"Let's go now," Sam called. "I'll carry Mini. Ben, you take the cubs. And Bessie, you carry the empty pail and the one with water in it. In case we get thirsty again on the way home."

Ben joined Sam at once, but Bessie lingered behind. Something had caught her eye. "Wait!" Her hand swept the bottom of the creek.

Curious, the boys turned to watch.

Bessie skipped toward them, her hand held high, her fingers wrapped so tightly around her treasure, they began to tingle.

"You found *gold?*" Ben asked, his eyes wide with surprise.

"Something better. Look."

"It's a penny." Sam was puzzled. "But it doesn't look like any penny I ever saw. It's so big."

On the front of the copper penny was a woman's head, her hair pulled back in a double bun. She wore a coronet, on her head, in which was inscribed the word LIBERTY. Thirteen six-pointed stars circled the word. At the bottom of the coin was a date — 1819. The back of the coin bore the words THE UNITED STATES OF AMERICA. In the center, enclosed in a laurel wreath, were the words ONE CENT.

"Is it real?" Ben asked.

"It sure is." Bessie danced around the boys. "It's a

real penny, and it's mine." She could see the glass case in Rosie's store. Her mouth watered. She wouldn't take the first candy to catch her eye. No, she would take a lovely long while to make a decision. The image of those treats made her anxious to get back even more quickly. They would go to Doc's place first. Then . . .

"Want me to hold the penny for you?" Sam offered.

Bessie shook her head. A dream captured could be a dream lost. She wanted that coin where she could see it every minute. She looked down into the pail that held the water. That was a good place, a wonderful place. She could see the penny clearly when she dropped it in.

Refreshed, the three walked a little more quickly.

"We're almost there," Sam said at last. When the familiar house came into view, they broke into a run, anxious now to have the long trek over.

They found Doc Hawkins out back, mending a fence. He didn't turn when he heard their voices, concentrating on his work.

"That's to make sure Pegasus and her colt don't get back into the marsh," Sam explained to Ben.

"I know," Ben said. "They could get hurt real bad."

Bessie was surprised Ben remembered. One time he had left the gate open, not on purpose, but because something else had caught his attention. Doc had been furious; the tongue-lashing he had given Ben had made Ben cringe. Hard words cut Ben deep; maybe those kind of words he couldn't forget.

Doc turned now to greet them, saw Mini on Sam's shoulders, and came running.

"What is it? What's happened?"

"We found Mini caught in a trap —"

"My pa set it," Ben interrupted. This, too, Ben remembered. And remembering brought shadows back into his eyes.

"And we found these cubs." Bessie pointed to the pails Ben held. "The mother fox was dead."

Doc Hawkins lifted Mini gently from Sam's shoulders. "Bring the cubs."

They followed him into the house, past a short hall and into his examining office. There he now placed Mini on the table and probed her wound with careful, skillful fingers.

"She was lucky," he said at last. "She's badly torn, but she'll heal."

He tended to her while the children watched closely, explaining as he worked what he was doing and why. When he began to stitch the wound, Ben walked away quickly and stared out the window, holding his fists clenched together. He turned back only when he heard Doc lift Mini and take her from the room.

"Now let's have a look at your bruises," Doc said.

He made them wash their hands with soap and rinse them thoroughly. Then he took a bottle from one of the shelves.

"No iodine!" Bessie gave him a wary look and thrust her hands behind her back. "That hurts."

"It will only sting for a minute."

Sam and Ben pressed their lips together when the iodine burned their palms. Bessie jumped and said accusingly, "I told you it would hurt."

At last Doc Hawkins turned his attention to the two cubs.

"You found the mother fox dead?" he asked as he placed the cubs on the table. "Here, Sam, hold this one down while I examine the other."

Ben came close, to see what Doc Hawkins was doing.

As Doc worked, he explained, "These cubs are in weak condition. They appear to be about two months old. Must have been born a little later than usual."

He glanced at Bessie's worried face. "Did you know that they're blind at birth? Their coats aren't thick and furry, just fine down."

"Like a duck," Bessie said.

"Not exactly. They don't open their eyes until they're ten days old, and when they do, what color do you think they are?"

"Brown," Sam said at once.

"Blue-gray. It's only later that the eyes turn to an amber brown."

Bessie was enchanted. A fox with blue eyes?

"I'll have to keep them. They're too young and frail to be turned loose now," Doc Hawkins said.

"I could take care of them." Bessie loved the feeling of their fur under her hands. "We don't have a pet. Except Mini," she added. "And she isn't really ours."

"I'm sorry, Bessie. These animals belong in the wild. Tell you what," he went on, seeing how unhappy she was. "Come back after supper, and I'll let you ride Pegasus."

Bessie couldn't believe he was saying that. Doc never let anyone ride Pegasus.

Doc looked at Ben and Sam. "All of you did such a wonderful thing, rescuing Mini from the trap like that. Saving the cubs. You can all have a turn on Pegasus."

They were so excited, Bessie forgot, until they were halfway home, that she had wanted to go to Rosie's.

"We can't," Sam explained. "Ma won't know what happened to us."

"Soup." Ben's face was bright with expectation. "With my mushrooms."

Now that Ben mentioned the soup, Bessie realized she was famished.

"Okay. Soup," she agreed. "And then I'll go to Rosie's."

"No," Sam told her firmly. "Then we pick blueberries. You and Ben and me."

Bessie got what Ma called her "mulish" look. Then she sighed. Getting that Erector Set was important to Sam. But tomorrow, she promised herself, as soon as they brought the bread and pies and muffins to Rosie's, she would pursue her dream.

Sam started to empty the pail that held the water. Bessie reached down and snatched her penny and shook her head when Sam offered to save it for her.

"It's *my* penny. I'll hold it."

Swinging their pails, Ben and Sam grinned at one another as they all headed for home.

"No use talking to her, now that she's rich," Sam told Ben.

Bessie didn't care. She *was* rich. Tonight she would ride Pegasus. And tomorrow she would buy real storemade candy!

7

Shadows at Dusk

They burst into the house, overflowing with their news.

Mrs. Kobb held up her hand. "Hold on. I can't make head nor tail out of what you're saying, with everyone talking at once. You start, Sam."

So Sam began. "Rosie had this Erector Set —"

"You left out about the summer man wanting to buy Pegasus," Bessie objected.

Sam frowned. "I'm trying to say what's important. Ma, you know how I've always wanted an Erector Set. Ever since Pa promised —"

"Yes. I remember." Mrs. Kobb's face took on that wistful expression she had when mention of the days when Pa had been home came up.

"Well, Rosie said I could have it for twelve dollars."

"*Twelve dollars?*" Mrs. Kobb repeated in a shocked voice.

"Wait, Ma. Listen. Rosie will take it in trade, sort of. Five cents for each pail of blueberries I pick. I figure I can make two dollars a week. The Erector Set — it's not like it's a *toy*," Sam continued anxiously. "It's something to start building with, Ma."

Mrs. Kobb thought it over for a moment. "You're not to neglect your chores. I won't have that," she warned.

Sam relaxed. Then he added, "Ben and Bessie are going to help, too."

"How much help? I know you, Sam. I know how you can be when you've set your mind to something."

"Only when they want to. Honest."

Bessie and Ben nodded. Then Bessie told her mother about looking for Mini and finding the fox cubs and her lucky penny. Mrs. Kobb examined the coin and gave it back to Bessie with a smile.

Bessie seized the opportunity, while her mother was in such a good mood, to say casually, "And Rosie had these gloves on the counter."

"You can use a good pair of woolen mittens for the winter. How much did Rosie want for them?" Mrs. Kobb caught the quick glance brother and sister exchanged. "What aren't you telling me?" she asked. Her lips tightened when Bessie described the gloves. "When would you *wear* them?" Mrs. Kobb shook her head in disapproval. And when Sam mentioned how much they would cost, Mrs. Kobb was stunned. "One dollar and twenty-five cents? For gloves? I'm sorry, Bessie. It would be different if money made no nevermind, but it does, and we have to be practical."

Bessie thought the word "practical" had to be the ugliest one in the English language.

"You didn't tell the best part of all," Ben reminded them. "We get to ride on Pegasus after supper. For saving Mini. And the cubs."

"The three of you? On Pegasus? Who would have believed it?" Mrs. Kobb said in wonder. "I must see this. I have to deliver five blueberry pies to Rosie after supper. I'll come with you. From Rosie's we can walk over to Doc Hawkins' place."

As soon as lunch was over, Sam announced it was time to pick blueberries. With pails swinging back and forth, they set out for the bushes closest to home. It would be kind of fun, Bessie told herself, picking berries, watching the pails fill up, knowing each pail would move Sam closer to getting the Erector Set.

"No twigs, no leaves, no hard green little berries," Sam reminded them.

It seemed to go quickly at first; there were berries to spare. Bessie hummed, and picked, and ate.

Sam was horrified. "You put each and every berry in that pail, not your mouth, Bessie Kobb," he ordered.

Bessie sighed. Berries were so sweet and juicy when they came fresh from the bush. But Sam was right.

The pile of berries grew, but movements slowed as they had to reach in for the fruit hidden in the bushes.

Soon their hands were marked with small scratches.
Insects stung their faces and arms. A small harmless
garden snake startled Bessie when it slithered across
her foot. She dropped her pail and stared angrily as
the berries spilled out on the ground.

"Dumb old snake," she whispered in a fury as she
kneeled down to gather up the berries. She tried to be
careful, but some leaves found their way into the pail
as well. She gave Sam a furtive look. Nobody can pick
just perfect berries, she told herself rebelliously. She
let the leaves remain.

Ben was distracted when a butterfly took wing from

his bush. He placed his pail carefully on the ground, then silently chased the delicate brown-edged yellow wings as they went gleaming from branch to branch.

Sam watched with brooding eyes but said nothing. His lips tightened with determination. He picked steadily as he worked his way in and out of each bush.

"I'm tired," Bessie said at last. "I don't want to pick anymore."

Sam started to object, looked at Bessie's drooping shoulders, and agreed. "It's been a long day. Let's quit."

"And we don't want to be too tired to ride Pegasus," Bessie told him.

"Ben," Sam shouted. "Let's go."

When they reached the Kobb house, Ben handed his half-full pail to Sam. "I've got to get home to do the chores, or Pa will be real mad."

"Come back after supper," Sam reminded him.

And Ben did come back, an angry red welt across his left cheek, and his gray eyes clouded in misery.

When Sam started to exclaim, his mother silenced him with a shake of the head. She applied a cold cloth to the bruise, and said in a matter-of-fact voice, "I saved a nice piece of pie for you, Ben."

Ben put his arms around Mrs. Kobb, and rested his head against her, eyes closed. "I wish I had a ma like you," he whispered.

Sam's hands clenched into fists, as if he wished he

could strike Mr. Tobin for hurting Ben. Bessie's eyes filled with unshed tears. She thought, Pa may be sick, and he may not be here just when we need him, but he is a loving man. He had always been a loving man. Even the war hadn't changed that.

By the time they left the house that evening, Ben's eyes were smiling again. Bessie skipped ahead, as she usually did, but Sam and Ben walked quietly on either side of Mrs. Kobb, Ben proudly holding the basket of pies. As soon as the pies were delivered to Rosie, they walked more quickly.

"It's later than we expected," Mrs. Kobb apologized to Doc Hawkins, but he brushed that aside.

"I'm just glad you could come." He led them around to the back of the house.

"I just love this time of day," Mrs. Kobb said.

Bessie knew what her mother meant. As the long summer day moved into evening, a peaceful hush closed in, a quiet broken only by the first chirping of crickets, and a small breeze whispering among the leaves. Even Pegasus, nibbling grass near the back fence, was tranquil as an evening star. And Jupiter, usually frisky and playful, was content to stand still except for a small swishing of his tail.

"I see you haven't finished that fence yet," Mrs. Kobb observed.

Doc Hawkins shook his head. "That little barrier

I've put up will keep them away. I just can't seem to find the time to get the fence done."

While the adults talked, Ben disappeared. Bessie and Sam smiled knowingly at each other.

"I bet that he's gone to see Mini," Bessie said.

In a few moments, Ben rejoined them. "You know what? I think those fox cubs know me. They licked my hands and my face. I wish I could keep them. I even know what I would call them," he added wistfully.

Bessie studied him. How Ben loved animals. The only one that didn't respond to him was Mr. Tobin's dog, Buddy Boy, who was strictly a one-man dog. "The fox cubs aren't pets," Bessie reminded Ben. "Remember what Doc told us? They're creatures of the wild. They have to go back to the woods when they can."

Doc Hawkins, who had heard Ben, now squeezed his shoulder gently. "It's time for me to saddle up Pegasus so you all can ride her." He whistled. Pegasus lifted her head, then came trotting obediently across the grass. Jupiter romped around her.

As Doc Hawkins walked toward the barn, both horses followed, heads bobbing up and down.

Pegasus was like captured sunshine. Jupiter was a rich chestnut brown shot through with gold. A white diamond shape stretched from just above his eyes, narrowing down like a pointer to his nose. His lower legs were white, but his hoofs were light brown.

"Aren't horses beautiful?" Bessie cried. "Don't you just love them?"

When Doc Hawkins returned, he led only Pegasus. Jupiter was in his stall for the night. As man and horse approached, Doc Hawkins called out, "You first, Sam."

When Sam was firmly in the saddle, his face exploded into a wide grin. "It feels funny. Not like I expected at all. But it's great!"

Doc Hawkins showed Sam how to hold the reins, then walked beside Pegasus as she moved carefully, round and round the entire enclosure.

Soon it was Bessie's turn. "Go like the wind," Bessie whispered. "Fly, Pegasus. Fly!" Bessie closed her eyes. Riding Pegasus was better than leaping from the hill with the umbrella. Someday, she dreamed, I'll climb on your back, Pegasus, and we'll dance our way through the clouds.

When the ride was over, Bessie came down reluctantly into Doc Hawkins' arms.

"Now me," Ben said, his eyes aglow. "You don't have to walk with me, Doc. Pegasus knows me. We'll be fine."

Doc Hawkins nodded.

In the west, the sun hurled a blaze of fiery color before it set. Overhead, dusk had deepened. Against the darkening sky, as Ben and Pegasus reached the far side of the field, they stood briefly silhouetted, shadow joined to shadow.

Then Pegasus began to dance. Bessie, half dreaming, was certain that Pegasus' feet no longer touched the ground but floated in a soft, gliding movement, her mane bouncing gently. And Ben, flinging a hand upward in a sweep of joy, surely had brushed the sky with his fingertips.

8

Sad Summer Song

Next morning, as soon as Bessie heard her mother stirring below, her eyes popped open. She needed no one to wake her today. She sat up, hugged her knees, and smiled at the world outside her window. Tomorrow had come!

She caroled her way down the steps, offered to help Sam bring coal up from the cellar, and helped her mother whip the eggs for the bread. She was long finished with breakfast while Sam was still eating.

"Can't you hurry up?" She tapped her foot impatiently.

"We have to wait for Ben anyway," he reminded her.

Bessie flung open the screen door, ready to race to the road, and almost careened into Ben.

"Hey!" Ben was startled. "You almost knocked the flowers out of my hands."

Bessie looked at the bouquet of weeds Ben held.

Who but Ben would think of weeds as flowers, she marveled. The bouquet was for Ma, of course. Each morning Ben brought her a gift. Sometimes it was mushrooms he picked in the woods, or berries, or pine cones, or delicate leaves. At times he gave her something he whittled. Ben wasn't school-smart, but he had clever hands.

"We have to get going," Bessie explained. "My ma said I could spend my penny and get anything I want."

Ben licked his lips. "Get the syrup bottles."

The syrup bottles were made of wax and shaped like tiny milk bottles. They were filled with small amounts of different colored liquids. To get at the syrup, you had to bite off the tops and then tip your head way back to drink.

"That's what I'd get if I had a penny," Ben said.

"Well, it's my penny and I get to choose what I want." She hoped Sam and Ben wouldn't expect to share. She patted the pocket in her dress. The penny was safe there, wrapped inside a handkerchief.

Sam was ready at last. Bessie grabbed her basket and set out at a rapid pace.

"Where's the fire?" Sam called, but she ignored him. All the way to Rosie's, Bessie sorted out the candies in her mind. She didn't wake from her daydream until the sound of Doc Hawkins' harmonica caught her attention. Pegasus was already dancing when the three of them arrived at the store. As usual, Ben and Sam brought their baskets inside. Then Ben took Bessie's basket while she danced with Pegasus.

What would the day be like without Pegasus, Bessie wondered as she twirled and pirouetted on the dusty road. But as soon as the music stopped, she forgot Pegasus in her hurry to go into the store.

Sam rushed in after her. "Make it quick, Bessie. Pick something, will you, and let's go."

"I can't rush. This is important," she began, then stopped when she saw the summer man. He paid no attention to her, however, just stared at the door expectantly. Bessie turned to see who was there. It was only Doc Hawkins.

"Rosie," Bessie shouted, working the penny clear of the handkerchief. "Look what I've got. A penny!"

"That's too big for a penny. Give it here and let me take a good look at it." Rosie squinted at the coin, then read the date. "Eighteen-nineteen!" she exclaimed. "Do you know how old this is?"

"Sure." Sam was quick with numbers. "It's one hundred and four years old."

Bessie's heart sank. "Oh. Is it still good?" she asked uncertainly.

"Where did you get it?" Rosie wanted to know.

"I found it. In Felton's Creek. Finders keepers. It's mine, isn't it?"

"Tell you what, Bessie. It's got to be worth something. I'll give you a quarter for it." Rosie opened the drawer under the counter, pulled out her cigar box, opened it, and searched for a quarter.

Bessie was stunned. A quarter? For a penny?

"Just a minute," the summer man said. "I'd like to look at that penny." He examined both sides, then turned to Bessie.

"I'll give you a dollar for it, little girl."

"Hold your horses," Rosie interrupted, annoyed. "She was talking to me."

"Never mind, Rosie. She'll take the dollar." Sam nudged his sister sharply. "Go ahead. Don't just stand there."

But Bessie couldn't move. How had a penny become a *dollar* so suddenly?

"I'll take it for her," Sam put in quickly, afraid the summer man might change his mind.

The summer man slipped the coin in his change pocket and handed the dollar to Sam.

"How lucky can you get?" Sam whispered to Bessie. Then, delighted, he shouted, "The first dollar for the Erector Set, Rosie. Now we only need eleven more."

Bessie spun around, furious. "That's my dollar."

Her brother was surprised. "But Bessie, don't you see? Now we won't have to pick as many blueberries."

"I don't care about your dumb old blueberries. I

don't care about your dumb old Erector Set, either. I wanted to choose my candy," she sobbed.

"Is that what the fuss is all about?" The summer man turned to Rosie. "Give the little girl five cents worth of . . ." He paused, then waved his hand. "Just throw five cents worth into a bag."

Rosie slid the glass door back. Her hand dipped into five trays, one after the other. Bessie didn't watch. She kept her head turned away, nor did she look when the summer man put the bag in her hand.

"There you are," the summer man said. "Problem solved."

"Aren't you going to see what Rosie gave you?" Ben whispered.

Bessie shook her head.

Now the summer man spoke to Doc Hawkins. "Step over to the counter, Doc. I've got something to show you."

Doc Hawkins waited a moment, and studied the other man's face. Then he stepped toward the counter. Bessie, Ben, and Sam crowded closer. Behind the counter, Rosie regarded the summer man suspiciously.

The summer man began to pull money out of his pockets, slapping them to make sure nothing remained.

"Hundred-dollar bills. For a total of three thousand

dollars. More than you make in a year, I imagine, Doc. Don't tell me you can't use the money to fix up your place. Fill in the marsh behind your broken fence. Get a new roof for your barn —"

"That's more than I paid for my house." Doc Hawkins made no move to touch the money, just stared at it, shaking his head.

Bessie looked down at her bag of candies. It would happen to Doc Hawkins, too. Suddenly, it had become a world in which a penny turned into a dollar, and horses turned into hundred-dollar bills.

"Feel it," the summer man urged Doc Hawkins. "See what real money feels like."

When Doc Hawkins replied, his voice was harsh. "You just don't understand, do you? Pegasus is special to me. She was my boy's horse. He taught her to dance."

"No disrespect intended, Doc. But your son's been dead now more than five years. At least that's what I heard. And there is an awful lot you could do with the money. Pick it up, man."

Doc Hawkins pressed his lips together, as if to keep angry words from spilling out. Then he said, quietly, "Follow me, sir. I want you to see something."

The summer man scooped up the money and stuffed it back in his pockets before he followed. Bessie and Ben and Sam trailed behind. Even Rosie hastened to leave the store.

Doc Hawkins stood at the top of the steps and pulled out his harmonica. Instead of the sprightly tunes he usually played, he began a melody soft as tears on a child's face and sad as a hurt that can't be healed.

Pegasus tipped her head and listened. Then she moved. It was a quiet dance, with small, delicate steps. The tapping sound of her hoofs against the road became part of the music. Her golden mane streamed gently in the faint breeze. She glowed in the sunlight, and if she had suddenly spread wings and flown away, it would have seemed natural.

Bessie turned to watch the people on the steps. Doc Hawkins' expression matched the music — sad, withdrawn, haunted. Rosie stood frozen, her hands clasped tight against her throat. Sam seemed to be looking off into the distance, taller, reaching into the future. Ben dreamed; the dream was in his wide gray eyes, as though he were here and elsewhere at the same time. The summer man took a deep breath and held it, then slowly let it go. His hands tightened against the money in his pockets and slowly came out, dangling and empty.

Bessie carefully placed her bag of candies on the ground. Then she joined Pegasus. She didn't swirl or dip or frolic as usual. Instead, she swayed back and forth, her eyes half-closed, her hands clutching her arms.

At last the music stopped. Doc Hawkins put the harmonica in his pocket and turned to the summer man. "That's why she's not for sale," he said, quietly. He went down the steps.

"Come on, Pegasus." He stroked her nose. "Let's go home."

Horse and man walked together, old friends who were comfortable with one another.

Bessie went up the steps to the summer man and handed him her bag of candy.

Startled, he looked down. "You can keep that, little lady."

"No." Her voice was so low he had to bend down to hear her. "I can't keep it."

Slowly she went down the steps again.

The summer man didn't understand, Bessie thought. He would never understand. She had longed to press her nose against the glass, to make the wonderful, agonizing decision about which candy she wanted. It had been important to her to make her own choice. He had taken that away.

Sam took her hand. "Listen, Bessie. You can have the dollar back. I had no right to grab it away from you. I'm sorry."

Bessie pushed the dollar away. "It's okay. I don't want it. You keep it for the Erector Set."

"We could take a penny from the dollar and you could still choose," he urged.

Bessie shook her head. "It wouldn't be the same anymore." She looked over her shoulder at the summer man, who didn't seem to know what to do next.

"He spoiled it," Bessie said.

She moved away from Sam and then, suddenly, began to run down the road as fast as she could.

9

The Blueberry Rebellion

"I'm so mad I could spit," Bessie shouted.

Sam stared at her. "What's the matter with you? What did I say?"

"You just give orders all the time, that's what's the matter. And pushing. All the time pushing us to work harder."

"Well, we didn't pick nearly enough blueberries yesterday. You know that."

"I don't care. And I'm not picking blueberries today. I'm tired of picking them. That's all we ever do anymore."

Sam's face reddened; his voice grew cold. "Just you wait a minute, Bessie Kobb."

"No. You wait a minute. We're not your slaves."

Ben stepped back. Harsh, angry words worried him. He glanced from Sam to Bessie and back again. Then he tried to soothe Bessie. "Well, see, we have to, because Sam says —"

Bessie flared up again. "We don't have to do anything. Sam never asked if we wanted to pick blueberries, did he? And he's never once thanked us, either. He's the one who wants the Erector Set, not us. Well, I don't care if he gets it or not. We've been picking blueberries for five weeks now —"

"Hardly four," Sam corrected.

Bessie glared at him. "So? It feels like five. It feels like forever. Summer used to be fun. Now it's just work, work, work."

She pressed her lips together grimly to keep from crying, then marched away from the boys, her head high and defiant.

She had been going to complain about Sam to her mother, but Pa had suddenly taken a turn for the worse, and Ma had spent mornings baking, afternoons at the sanatorium, and evenings staring into space, withdrawn and grieving and silent.

It had been the longest month of Bessie's life. If only she could have talked to Ma, but how could she burden her now? So Bessie often cried herself to sleep, and woke up dispirited to each new day.

It was all too much. She couldn't help Pa, or Ma, for that matter. But she could do without Sam and his everlasting blueberries.

Sam said in a loud voice, so Bessie could hear every word, "We don't need her, Ben. She's only a kid, anyway. Come on, Ben. Let's go."

"Go ahead. Go with him. I don't need you, either," Bessie whispered to herself.

She pounded along the road, racing home, not to speak to her mother, but to get Pa's big black umbrella. As she ran, she turned her face up to let the freshening breeze wash over her. She'd never pick another blueberry again, she vowed. She might never even eat one again.

When she reached the house, she stopped and glanced toward it warily. Her mother was nowhere to be seen. Stepping softly, she climbed the few steps to the front porch, lifted the umbrella from its stand near the door, and tiptoed down again, almost tripping over Ben.

"You scared me. What are you doing here, anyway? How come you didn't go with Sam? You always do what he wants."

"I thought maybe you were crying." He looked at her anxiously. "Are you mad at me, too?"

She shook her head. How could anyone be angry with him? "I'm going to the cliff. You want to come?"

Bessie turned her head, listening for her mother's footsteps. "Quick, Ben, Ma is coming to the front door. Let's go before she sees us."

They fled down the steps, across the road, and into the woods. Neither one saw Mrs. Kobb on the porch, staring after them thoughtfully.

The cliff to which Bessie led them rose from a flat sandy area. Just beyond lay a strawberry patch where Bessie and Ben picked berries so Ma could make shortcakes and tarts and pies. The cliff was a small hill, one side of which seemed to have been sliced off with a giant knife. Although it was only about an eight-foot drop from the top to the ground, it felt much farther to Bessie when she teetered on the edge of the cliff.

Bessie waited until Ben went down the narrow path on the side of the hill and stationed himself below. When he was there, Bessie wet her finger and held it aloft to see in which direction the wind was blowing. Pa had taught her to do that. He was the one who showed her how to jump from the cliff. He had always waited below, just where Ben was, to catch her and break her fall.

Bessie sniffed the air, and raised her face to let the breeze caress her. Then she opened the umbrella.

The wind whistled in under the open umbrella, lifting it in the air with a quick surge. Bessie's feet no longer touched the ground. For one long, beautiful moment, Bessie flew. Then the weight of her body tugged the umbrella downward. She fell like a bird with folded wings, but first she had soared!

Ben caught her easily. "Can I fly now? Please, Bessie?"

Bessie started to shake her head, saw his pleading look, and said, "Sure."

Ben's face was radiant. She had never let him jump before. Afraid she might change her mind, he seized the umbrella, ran round the hill, and raced to the top. There he opened the umbrella, leaped, and plummeted to the ground. For a moment, he didn't move.

"Ben!" Bessie shook him, screaming in his ear. "Ben. Please. Don't be dead!"

She was just about to leave to find help when Ben stirred at last. She helped him sit up. He glanced up, then down. He was bewildered. "Did I get to fly?"

He sounded so anxious she said, "Yes, Ben. You did."

"I don't remember." He frowned. "Should I try again?"

"No, Ben. You're too big."

"Are you going to try again?"

But Bessie had lost heart. Ben's fall had started her thinking again.

Sam had changed. He was so busy with his blueberries and Erector Set, he had no time for summer joys anymore. He hadn't even given another thought to Mini and the cubs. But Ben had kept them in mind always. Each morning, after the breads and other baked goods had been delivered to Rosie, Ben had darted off to Doc Hawkins' place.

79

Bessie had followed him several times, to find Ben walking Mini patiently and then, when she could, encouraging her to run. He had talked earnestly to the cubs in a soft lilting tone to which they seemed to pay keen attention.

And just two days ago, when Doc Hawkins announced he was ready to release the cubs, who suddenly weren't babies anymore, Sam was indifferent.

"You can go along if you want," Sam told them. "I'm too busy."

So it was that Bessie and Ben accompanied Doc Hawkins to turn the cubs loose in the woods. They had scampered off, bursting with energy and the joy of freedom. They had turned back for a moment to frolic around Ben. Then, without a backward glance, they disappeared into the woods.

Bessie could almost see the lump that rose in Ben's throat, and feel the ache that made Ben twist his hands mournfully.

Bessie had been sad then, and she was sad now. Sam had no time for summer joys. Soon she wouldn't be able to fly anymore. That's what Sam had forgotten, that their summer days and summer dreams would soon be behind them.

"Let's get the canoe and go out on the lake," Bessie suggested impulsively.

Once again, they approached the house, where

Bessie tiptoed up the steps, replaced the umbrella, and then put a cautionary finger to her lips. Smiling, she and Ben fled behind the house and escaped into the woods.

The canoe was moored at a point on the lake beyond where the summer children played. The sun was high and hot, but they skirted the lake close to the shore, under the shade of weeping willows and maple trees in full leaf. From afar, the laughter of the summer children was muted; Ben and Bessie moved gently on the water, silent shadows drifting in a pocket of peace.

"Indians used to live around this lake." Bessie's voice was low. "Sam said they used to go back and forth on this lake in birch-bark canoes. We used to pretend we were Indians. We used to . . ." She stopped. Why did it all sound so long ago?

So many things were different. First Pa left, and Ma stepped in to fill his place as well as her own. Now Sam was reaching out hard for his future; the Erector Set was just the first of many steps to come. Ma said it was natural; Sam was growing up. But he was growing up fast, and leaving Bessie behind.

Suddenly she wanted to go home. "Turn the canoe around, Ben."

Obedient to her wish, Ben swung his paddle to the other side of the canoe and maneuvered it around for the return journey.

Bessie sighed. Why did she have such mixed-up feelings? She loved Sam and admired him. Her mother was right. Sam had been forced to grow up too fast when Pa went to the sanatorium. Sam had worked and worked and never complained. He deserved to have the Erector Set, and it was only fair and just that she should help him.

But summer was slipping away — the lazy, drifting days of summer were vanishing. Didn't Sam miss them at all?

Pa once told her that a little rebellion was good for the spirit. Maybe so. But it would be mean-hearted to stop now, when Sam was so close to his goal.

Bessie sighed again. She knew that her blueberry rebellion was over.

10

A Member of the Family

They came back to the house just in time for lunch. Sam was already there, his elbows on the table, his chin resting on his fists. He didn't look up as they joined him.

"Something's going on around here, and I want to know what it is." Mrs. Kobb stood with her arms folded, and waited.

"Could we just eat first, Ma? I'm starved," Bessie said. She sniffed. "I smell potatoes, and onions . . ."

". . . and dill and celery," Ben put in helpfully.

Mrs. Kobb spoke sharply. "I know what's in the soup. Sam!"

He raised his head, carefully looking away from his sister and Ben.

"We'll start with you. Now."

"They just got tired of picking blueberries. That's all."

"I expect there was more to it than that."

You couldn't fool Ma, Bessie thought. She wondered how her mother was able to read their minds
just by looking at their faces.

"You first," Ma told Bessie, and listened with compressed lips and angry eyes as Bessie told her mother about her rebellion. As his sister spoke, Sam grew more and more uncomfortable. He dropped his head and stared blindly at the floor.

"Why didn't you come to me right away?" Mrs. Kobb asked, when Bessie stopped speaking. "Why did you wait so long?"

"I couldn't bother you while Pa was so sick, Ma. But now that Pa is better . . ." Bessie broke off, then asked anxiously, "He is better, isn't he?"

Mrs. Kobb's hand flew up to cover her lips. Then she clenched her hands together and shook her head. "That was wrong of me, and I'm sorry. Pa is very important to me, but so are you children. Yes. Pa is better. But better or worse, I'll never neglect you again. Never."

She turned to Sam. "I can't believe that any son of mine would turn into a bully."

Sam was shocked. "MA!"

"Yes, a bully," she repeated firmly. "And what's worse, someone looking only to his own interest. That's not how we are in this family, and don't you ever forget it."

Ben flinched away from the fury in Mrs. Kobb's voice, but she disregarded him.

"Here and now, you apologize, Sam Kobb!"

Sam said quickly, "I do, Ma. I'm truly sorry."

"Don't tell me. Tell them," she replied, her face still cold.

Ben squirmed in his chair uneasily. "He doesn't have to. I like helping Sam. Honest I do. He's my best friend in the whole world."

Mrs. Kobb's expression softened as she looked at Ben. "I'm glad to hear that," she told him. "But saying sorry isn't good enough. Sam will have to settle now how much he's going to pay you and Bessie."

Bessie was shocked. She wished now she had never rebelled. It bothered her to see her brother looking so miserable. "Come on, Ma," she said. "He doesn't have to pay me. I'm his sister."

"Sam is earning twelve dollars . . . eleven dollars," Mrs. Kobb said, remembering Bessie's dollar. "So he is being paid for his work. You and Ben are putting in as much time and work as Sam —"

"But, Ma," Sam interrupted, his face pale with anxiety, "I won't be able to get the Erector Set then for another week, maybe two."

In spite of the fact that neither Bessie nor Ben wanted to be paid, Mrs. Kobb insisted. "What's fair is fair," she said.

"We don't get paid for the chores we do, and bringing the bread and stuff to Rosie's every day." Bessie was puzzled.

"That's different. That's family pulling together for family, and nobody getting more than his share."

"How much shall I pay them?" Sam asked. "I've never had to pay anybody before."

"Ask them what they want," Mrs. Kobb suggested and returned to the stove, where soup simmered, ready to be served.

Ben thought and thought, then his eyes lit up in expectation. "I know. Can I have your kazoo?"

Sam was taken by surprise. "My kazoo? Don't you want money so you can buy something?" He glanced toward his mother uneasily. He was pleased Ben didn't want money, but it was only fair to explain. "Listen, Ben. It isn't even new. I found it near the lake last year where one of the summer kids threw it away. Remember?"

"I guess so," Ben answered.

"You have to remember. I made a kazoo out of tissue paper and my comb. I gave that to you when I found the kazoo."

The kazoo was a narrow tin tube with a small opening. If you blew or hummed into it, a tune vibrated with a buzzing sound out the other end.

"That's what I want," Ben insisted.

"Shake," Sam said, to seal the bargain. The boys gravely shook hands. Then Sam turned to Bessie. She was the one who had raised the rumpus.

"The first thing I want is one dollar and twenty-five cents." Bessie stared at Sam defiantly, then peered at her mother to see how she would react to Bessie's next words. "I want to get those white gloves."

"No, Bessie." Mrs. Kobb's voice was quiet but firm.

"But Ma," Bessie protested. "It's my own money. I ought to be able to do what I want with my own money."

"You don't have the right to throw it away. Money is too hard to come by, Bessie. Now if you want to look in the catalogue and get yourself a nice dress for school, or mittens —"

"Then you can keep the money, Sam. I don't care what you do with it." Bessie fought to keep tears from spilling down her cheeks. "Just give me a penny for candy. And I want you to let me look as long as I feel like it, and don't let anybody bother me while I'm looking." Bessie shot out the words all in one long breath.

She glared at her brother, then went on, "And when I choose, I don't want to have to share with anybody."

Mrs. Kobb winked at Sam over Bessie's head. "Give me a hand here, Sam." She ladled soup into a large bowl, which Sam carried carefully to the table and placed before Bessie.

"Friends again?" he whispered.

Bessie nodded and dug into her soup. Her mother

served Ben and Sam and was just about to ladle out soup for herself when the kitchen door was hurled open. It crashed against the wall, shaking the dishes in a cupboard nearby.

"You ever hear of knocking, Clay Tobin?" Mrs. Kobb's voice was frosty.

He ignored her and fastened his gaze on Ben.

"I knew I'd find you here. Always here, or over at Doc's place. Never at home when I need you. Scatterbrained, that's what you are, just like your ma. She never had the sense she was born with, either. Much help either one of you ever were with the farm. Well, now I've lost it, thanks to both of you. Couldn't meet the payments, and the bank's foreclosed. I don't know what the world's coming to if a man can't depend on his wife and his son."

Mrs. Kobb's lips tightened. Tillie Tobin had been a pretty woman at first, always fussing and primping. But Mr. Tobin was a bad-tempered husband and father, as free with his fists as he was with scornful words. One day Tillie Tobin had enough and ran away. Mrs. Kobb could understand that. What she couldn't forgive was her leaving Ben.

Ben sighed, a sound Mr. Tobin ignored. "I'm leaving. For good. I never could scratch out a living here and I'm sick of trying."

"But where will you go?" Mrs. Kobb disliked him,

but she knew he had tried hard to keep his small farm working. "And what about Ben? He can't be moving around from place to place —"

"I'm not taking the boy. He wouldn't want to come anyway, I expect. I haven't been much of a father to him, but then he isn't much of a son, is he? We're mismatched, you might say. There's no one to blame for it —"

"Not taking him?" Mrs. Kobb was outraged. "You're just going to walk out on him? On your own flesh and blood? He's only thirteen!"

"He can fend for himself. My pa turned me out when I was eleven. And I'm here to tell the tale." He turned to go.

"Just a minute," Mrs. Kobb said. "You may be washing your hands of him, but you're not leaving until you give me money to buy him some decent winter clothes. That's the least you can do."

"I can't spare a dime," Mr. Tobin began, but Mrs. Kobb went close to him and seized his shirt. Her face was flushed with anger; her eyes bored into Mr. Tobin.

"I'll have something for the boy if I have to strip you bare," she said.

Mr. Tobin laughed uneasily. "Hey, listen, I'm not fighting with no wild cat." He dug into his pocket and handed her a ten-dollar bill. Then, without another word, he went out, letting the screen door bang shut hard behind him.

Ben ran to the window. His father jumped into his truck with never a backward look. Waiting for him in the front seat was the dog, Buddy Boy.

Ben turned and stared at the others blindly. "He's taking Buddy Boy. He'd rather take his dog than me."

Sam scowled. "Never mind." He put his arm around Ben. "Look at it this way. You've got us, and Mini, and Pegasus."

Ben nodded, but his eyes were like Mini's when she had been caught in the trap, frightened and lost.

He's hurting bad, Bessie realized. Even though he said he hated his father, he was still hurting. On impulse, she went to him and twined his fingers in hers.

"Like Sam says, you have us, Ben. You'll always have us, won't he, Ma?"

Mrs. Kobb nodded. Before filling a bowl of soup for herself, she led Ben to the table. Then she stroked his head with a loving hand.

11

Oh, Pegasus

It was going to be a beautiful day, a wonderful day, a special day.

Bessie made a song of the words as she waited for her mother to come back to the kitchen.

"Is the cake ready? Can I see it?" Bessie asked eagerly. Ever since the day two weeks ago that Doc Hawkins had asked her mother to bake the cake, Bessie had been wondering what the cake would look like. Even her mother had been surprised at Doc Hawkins' request.

"I want it to be a real celebration," he had told Mrs. Kobb. "Pegasus will be ten years old."

"Do horses have birthdays? Just like people?" Bessie wondered.

"Pegasus isn't just a horse, Bessie. Is she, Doc?" Ben asked.

"She's special," Doc Hawkins agreed. "And that's why I want a special cake for the occasion."

Now Mrs. Kobb smiled at her daughter. "Close your eyes, Bessie." She nodded to the boys, who followed her to the pantry. There, on the long wooden table where Mrs. Kobb set her pies to cool, was a large oblong cake, colorfully iced in yellow and blue. It was on a wide board, set well away from the edges.

"Careful when you lift it, boys," Mrs. Kobb warned. She watched anxiously as they carried it into the kitchen.

"Oh, Ma! It's beautiful. Doc will just love it," Bessie cried. "I wish it didn't have to be cut up into pieces."

"You're an artist, Ma," Sam said with admiration. "I could never draw a horse like you did. And just with icing!"

Mrs. Kobb smiled with pleasure. She hadn't been sure it would turn out right. Even the yellow and blue wreath around the neck, with flowers and leaves interwoven, was perfect. Across the bottom of the cake, she had spelled out OUR PEGASUS.

It would be a surprise to everyone at Doc's.

Bessie ran to the door when she heard Doc Hawkins' truck pull up. When he came into the kitchen, he looked at the cake and shook his head. "This isn't a cake, Dora. It's a creation!"

"It's nice to do something just for fun," Mrs. Kobb told him.

Bessie didn't understand. Her mother was paid to

94

make the cake. How was it different from all the other baking she did?

The boys helped Doc bring the cake out to the truck, where they placed it on the floor in back. Ben sat on one side, and Sam on the other, to hold the cake steady. Mrs. Kobb and Bessie sat in front, Bessie near the open window to let her hair stream in the breeze.

"I've got a table set up in back," Doc said when they reached his house.

When the boys put the cake on the table, they expected to help set the dishes as well, but Mrs. Kobb waved them away.

"I can manage," she told them. "Today's a day just for you boys to relax and have fun."

The first guests to arrive were Grover Abbott from the farm next to the Hawkins place, and his son Ned.

"It's a wonderful day, isn't it?" Mrs. Kobb greeted them.

"It will be, soon as I get a slice of that cake," Grover Abbott said.

The Keefers — George Keefer, his wife, Molly, and the two boys, Luke and Purley — shouted a hello to Doc Hawkins. Mrs. Kobb shooed the boys away from the cake, though Purley managed to whip up some of the icing with a lightning-fast finger.

Rosie, in a dress of blinding red, white, and blue stripes, came just in time to shake a fist at Luke as he tried to sneak at the cake from behind Mrs. Kobb.

"George," Rosie shouted to their father, "can't you keep these boys out of mischief?"

"Boys will be boys," he shouted back jovially. "They're just high-spirited, is all."

Rosie muttered under her breath. "I'd high-spirit them, if they were mine."

"Relax, Rosie," Mrs. Kobb told her. "As soon as some of the other neighbors drift in with their kids, Luke and Purley will have someone to play with. Oh, look! Here comes Doc with Pegasus."

"And Jupiter never far behind." Rosie laughed. "Those two are a treat for the eyes."

The children had run toward Doc Hawkins, to stroke Pegasus lovingly. Even Luke and Purley reached up to run their hands across her face.

Doc Hawkins gave the reins to Ben.

"Walk her around slowly. It's her birthday, and everyone will want to see her. But don't let any of the children come too close to her."

Ben was delighted to be in charge. Gently, he urged Pegasus to follow him, staying close to the fence as he walked. Pegasus shied clear of the small barrier where Doc still hadn't finished repairing the break in the fence. Bessie walked with Ben, but Sam went to get some lemonade, and Luke and Purley raced ahead of him, whooping with joy in the hope of persuading

Mrs. Kobb to start slicing the cake.

Meanwhile, Doc tethered Jupiter to the fence.

Ben stared after the Keefer boys, his eyes troubled. "I wish they hadn't been invited."

"I know," Bessie agreed. "But they're neighbors. Doc had to ask them. Besides, some of the other neighbors will be here soon. Luke and Purley would never start anything with grown-ups here. Just let's keep on walking, okay?"

As they walked slowly on, they didn't notice Luke and Purley come racing up behind them, Purley still licking the icing he had snatched from the cake, and Luke grinning at finding Ben and Pegasus at the far end of the enclosure.

"Hey, Ben. Wait up," Luke called.

Ben swiveled his head sharply. "Now don't you start anything, Luke."

"Me?" Luke asked in an innocent voice. "I'm not doing anything, am I? Purley and me, all we want to do is take a ride on Pegasus."

"Forget it." Bessie clenched her hands into tight fists. "You leave us alone or I'll call your father."

"Your little mama taking care of you, Ben?" Luke put a finger on his chin and wiggled his shoulders back and forth.

Ben turned back. "I'll take Pegasus to the stable," he told Bessie. He pulled at the reins and began to move away swiftly. Bessie followed, ignoring Luke's taunts. With their backs to the boys, neither Ben nor Bessie was prepared for what happened next.

Luke and Purley whispered, then nodded in agreement. Glancing around to see if they were observed, they lit some firecrackers and tossed them at Ben.

"Early Fourth of July," Luke yelled.

"Yeah. We couldn't wait for tomorrow," Purley shouted.

The firecrackers exploded almost directly under Pegasus. Startled, Ben dropped the reins. Pegasus reared, her forelegs pawing the air, her eyes wild with fright. Her whinny carried clear across the field; at the fence, Jupiter snorted and pawed the ground as he tried to break loose.

"Did you see her jump?" Purley laughed as he tossed another firecracker.

This time Pegasus' cry was a high-pitched call of terror. The adults turned and stared in disbelief; Doc Hawkins shouted in rage when he saw Luke hurl another firecracker.

As Pegasus reared again in panic, Doc Hawkins came tearing across the field, closely followed by Grover Abbott, his son Ned, and George Keefer.

"We've got to stop her," Doc Hawkins cried. "She's heading for the marsh."

He was first to reach the fence, first to clear it.

"Pegasus! NO! STOP!" he called to her, but nothing could hold her back now. She raced ahead until, suddenly, her blind bolt ended as she hit the marsh and began to sink. Desperately she whipped her body around, struggled forward, managed to get her forelegs on solid ground. But the marsh was spongy and yielding and sucked her back legs deeper and deeper.

Pegasus panted; her head swung back and forth as

she tried to free herself.

Doc Hawkins reached her first, but the other men were close behind.

"We'll hang on to her as best we can," Ned said. "George, get some ropes from your truck."

George Keefer nodded and sped off. Meanwhile, Doc Hawkins advised, "Let's see if we can release her a little meanwhile."

The Abbotts and Doc Hawkins strained hard but made no headway.

"It's no use," Grover Abbott said. "We can't budge her without ropes. She's really stuck."

As soon as George Keefer came running back, the men looped strands of rope around Pegasus.

When this was done, Grover Abbott pointed out, "These ropes are rough, Doc. They're going to tear at her skin."

"Pull," Doc Hawkins replied grimly.

Luke and Purley had run back to stay close to their mother's side, pale-faced and frightened at the result of their mischief.

When the men had run in pursuit of Pegasus, Mrs. Kobb, Rosie, and Mrs. Keefer followed them as far as the fence, Mrs. Keefer holding her sons in an iron grip. Mrs. Keefer said, "If your pa doesn't take his belt to you, then I will."

Mrs. Kobb and Rosie had been shocked into silence. Then Rosie said impatiently, "I'm not going to stand here and wait to see what happens. The more hands the better. I'm going to help."

"So am I," Mrs. Kobb said with equal determination. "No," she added, as Mrs. Keefer started to join her, "you'd best stay here and put a leash on your boys."

Mrs. Kobb climbed over the fence, but Rosie walked to the gate, closed it behind her, and both made their way to where the men still struggled to set Pegasus free. Together, the women grasped one of the ropes. Doc Hawkins nodded his thanks.

"Let me help, too," a voice said. Doc Hawkins glanced up in surprise. It was the summer man.

"I know I wasn't invited to your party. But I wanted to see Pegasus again."

"You'll get your clothes dirty," Rosie said, staring at the summer man's white pants, his black-and-white shoes, his pink shirt.

"They're only clothes," the summer man said.

"Then grab a rope," Doc Hawkins told him. He tightened his own grasp on his rope. "Are we ready? Then all together. NOW. *Heave!*"

As the men pulled, the muscles in their arms corded into knots. The tendons in their necks swelled. Their faces turned scarlet. Several were gasping for breath.

Pegasus came free slowly. Quivering, she stood for

a moment, then sank to the ground. Doc Hawkins examined her carefully.

"She'll be all right, won't she, Doc?" the summer man asked anxiously.

Doc Hawkins shook his head. "She must have hit hard when she landed in the marsh. Both her front legs are broken."

"You're not going to put her down, are you?" The summer man spoke in a choked voice. "Not this beautiful creature." He glared at Doc Hawkins. "What a shame! She'd still be fine if you'd sold her to me. Now neither one of us will have her."

Doc Hawkins stared at him without expression. Then he patted Pegasus gently. "Steady, girl," he whispered. Tears glistened in his eyes. "Steady," he said again.

Grover kneeled beside him. "Doc, George brought his gun from the truck. You want me to . . ." He didn't finish, just waved at Pegasus.

Doc Hawkins kept his voice low. "It's all right, Grover. I'll take care of my girl."

Ben and Bessie and Sam had been pushed aside when the men had come to rescue the horse. Now Ben broke away from them and ran to Pegasus. Weeping, he stroked her head.

"Oh, Pegasus," he mourned.

Grover lifted Ben to his feet. "Come away, son," he

said kindly. "Give Doc his time with Pegasus."

Ben walked away slowly. At the sound of the shot, he stiffened, then tore away and ran back. Doc caught and held him.

"We'll bury her under that chestnut tree she loved so much, Ben." He turned Ben toward the fence and pointed. "Look, there's Jupiter. He's going to need someone to love him a lot now."

He pushed Ben gently. "Go take care of him. He's

frightened and skittish. Get him back in the stable, Ben. Will you do that for me?"

When Ben had raced back at the sound of the shot, Bessie and Sam had run after him. While Doc Hawkins spoke to Ben, they had stood silently aside. Now, at Doc Hawkins' nod, they joined him.

Together, the three of them began to walk slowly toward the frightened colt.

12

Endings and Beginnings

The blueberry picking days were over at last. Bessie and Sam and Ben had delivered the baked goods to Rosie. Now they stood by and waited for her to finish talking to the summer man. When he turned and saw the three children, he asked Ben, "How's Jupiter coming along?"

"He's fine. I take good care of him," Ben replied.

"And the dog? Is she up and about?"

"Mini's fine, too."

Bessie glanced at her brother. Sam was getting impatient. He had waited a long time for this day, but the summer man was in no hurry. "I thought I might see Doc Hawkins here this morning," he said to Rosie.

She shook her head. "He hasn't been in since . . ."

Since Pegasus died two weeks ago, Bessie thought. It had been hard to stop listening for the sound of Doc Hawkins' harmonica and Pegasus' hoofs tapping on the road. But she was gone, and Doc Hawkins had put away his harmonica.

"I wish everything was back the way it was," Bessie whispered.

The summer man shrugged. "It's what the fates decide, little girl." In a moment, he left, whistling under his breath.

"Now, what can I do for you?" Rosie pretended she didn't know what Sam and Bessie were waiting for.

"Sam wants his Erector Set," Ben cried.

"Bessie first," Sam said quickly.

She took a deep breath and edged her way to the candy case, clutching her penny. Rosie had already stationed herself there, waiting with a grin that made her cheeks fold over.

Bessie moved back and forth, undecided.

"Take your time, child." Rosie folded her fat arms on the case.

What should it be? Bessie asked herself. She pointed to the foxy grandpas and then quickly pulled her finger back. She hovered over the pralines, then moved on to the chocolate kisses, teetered in front of the candy buttons attached to long narrow strips of paper. She studied the rock candy, decided against that, and stared at the Tootsie Rolls. Then she simply closed her eyes, waved her forefinger in the air, and stabbed at the case.

"Good choice," Rosie said.

With her eyes still closed, Bessie asked, "What did I choose, Rosie?"

Rosie handed a small brown bag to Sam, who put it in his sister's hand.

"Look and see," he suggested.

Bessie opened her eyes, started to reach into the bag, and changed her mind. "I'll wait until I get home."

"How can you wait?" Ben wondered.

He didn't understand, Bessie told herself. She wanted to be alone in her room, open the bag very, very slowly, maybe just take a peek inside. No, maybe she would feel the bag first and try to guess what it held. After that, she would eat the candy, sitting on her bed, looking over the garden at the woods. A silent time, and all hers.

"Now," Rosie said. "It's your turn." Bessie and Ben crowded next to Sam at the counter. They watched silently as she reached up to the shelf on which the Erector Set had waited all these long weeks, and took it down. She wiped the box with her hand, then wiped her hand on her dress. She held the box a moment longer while she studied Sam's face. When she handed it to him finally, she said, "You earned it, Sam."

Sam clutched the box close to his chest. "We did it," he shouted. "We did it."

When Bessie saw the expression on Sam's face, she

was glad that she had helped. It hadn't been easy, and at times she had hated her brother, but now that was all in the past.

She edged closer to the counter, to see if the gloves were still there. Rosie studied Bessie but said nothing.

Sam, ready to leave, hugging his prize tightly, turned to call to his sister, but stopped short as he saw her reach out tentatively toward the gloves, then pull her hand back.

"We've got to go, Bessie," he said gently.

Bessie nodded. "I know." She set her lips firmly and walked away from the counter with determination. "At least you've got what you wanted," she told him.

"Thanks to you and Ben. I never could have done it without you, Bessie."

Bessie stared at him. "Yes you could. I think you'll always get what you want, Sam."

In the week that followed, Bessie was restless. Now that the blueberry picking was over, there was time to go to the lake, to watch the summer children and wonder what it was like to be a summer child.

There was time, too, for climbing the hill, to open the umbrella, to feel the wind lift her free.

But her spirits refused to soar.

Each day, with dragging feet, she made her way homeward.

"Bessie," Sam greeted her several days later, his eyes glowing. "Where were you? I've been waiting and waiting." His voice was filled with excitement.

Bessie stared at him, then at Ben, and finally at her mother.

"What's up, Ma?" she asked.

Mrs. Kobb shrugged. "I haven't the faintest notion."

"Everybody sit down," Sam ordered, "and close your eyes."

"Sam," Mrs. Kobb began, "I haven't got time —"

"For this you have time." Sam was firm. "Everybody sit."

Everyone waited expectantly, eyes squeezed shut.

"NOW!" Sam shouted.

Mrs. Kobb started up from her chair with a frown, saw Bessie's radiant face, and sank down in her chair again.

Ben drew a deep breath.

Bessie sat frozen in her chair. Then she whispered, "Sam. They're not for me. Are they?"

Sam pushed the box closer. There they were, the white satin gloves, with the delicate lace and the tiny pink pearls.

"I picked blueberries all week. By myself, Ma. And I mucked out the barn for Doc Hawkins. And I weeded Grover Abbott's vegetable garden."

"Just so you could get the gloves for me?" Bessie was stunned. She looked apprehensively at her mother, who hadn't uttered a word.

"For you. Because I know what it is to want something so bad it can make you heartsick." He turned to his mother. "Ma, you have to understand. There's got to be more than always being practical. There has to be room for dreams, too. Even if they seem foolish, or wasteful."

Mrs. Kobb watched as Bessie drew the gloves close, touched them with wonder, transformed from the listless child to one spilling over with gladness.

Mrs. Kobb's eyes misted with tears. "I guess you're never too old to learn, are you, Sam?" she asked in a husky voice. She cleared her throat, as if she had been sentimental too long. "Now you all shoo out of here. I've got work to do."

So they went to sit on the front steps, Bessie still clutching the gloves.

Bessie thought, Ma always said there was no use wishing for the impossible. But the impossible could happen, *had* happened!

Who would have dreamed she would find a valuable penny that would help Sam get his Erector Set? Sam had already built his first bridge with it. No matter what he built when he was grown, he'd probably always remember his first bridge, and the Erector Set.

She got her candy, though it seemed for a long time that dream wouldn't ever come true. And Sam had cared enough about her to work hard to get her the gloves. She might never wear them, but that didn't matter. Maybe someday, when she was grown, and married, with a daughter of her own, she would give the gloves to that child of the future. And tell her to dream. Bessie nodded, and hugged that thought to herself.

On impulse, she turned to Ben. "Sam got his Erector Set. And I got my candy. And these beautiful gloves. You're the only one who didn't get anything at all."

Ben's gray eyes grew luminous. "Oh yes I did, Bessie. I got you, and Sam, and Ma Kobb. I got a *family*, and I got love. I got the best of all."

Sam stood up, feeling restless. "Come on. Let's go down to the lake and go canoeing."

Sam and Ben raced ahead. Bessie drifted behind them, still lost in thought.

On the surface, everything seemed the same again, in some ways, even better. Ma hummed now when she worked, for Pa, though not cured, was well enough to come home for a while.

Mini was completely healed, though every once in a while she limped.

Doc Hawkins allowed them to ride freely on Jupiter, provided they took good care of him.

But everything wasn't the same.

Ben would disappear from time to time, to return with eyes stormy from weeping, remembering Pegasus. Sam would be absorbed in some chore, then suddenly lift his head and listen as the clip-clop of a horse's hoofs sounded clear on the air.

There would never be a summer like this again. For there could never be another Pegasus. She had

brought something special into their lives. Now her dancing days had ended. And Bessie would never again spin and twirl in the dust of a country road, to the tune of a harmonica, a dancing horse at her side.

Maybe, as she grew older, she would forget all the other things that had happened the year she was eight. But, Bessie told herself, as she ran to catch up with Sam and Ben, I'll always remember this time as the summer of the dancing horse.

APPLE® PAPERBACKS

Pick an Apple and Polish Off Some Great Reading!

BEST-SELLING APPLE TITLES

❑ MT43944-8	**Afternoon of the Elves** Janet Taylor Lisle	$2.75
❑ MT43109-9	**Boys Are Yucko** Anna Grossnickle Hines	$2.75
❑ MT43473-X	**The Broccoli Tapes** Jan Slepian	$2.95
❑ MT42709-1	**Christina's Ghost** Betty Ren Wright	$2.75
❑ MT43461-6	**The Dollhouse Murders** Betty Ren Wright	$2.75
❑ MT43444-6	**Ghosts Beneath Our Feet** Betty Ren Wright	$2.75
❑ MT44351-8	**Help! I'm a Prisoner in the Library** Eth Clifford	$2.75
❑ MT44567-7	**Leah's Song** Eth Clifford	$2.75
❑ MT43618-X	**Me and Katie (The Pest)** Ann M. Martin	$2.75
❑ MT41529-8	**My Sister, The Creep** Candice F. Ransom	$2.75
❑ MT42883-7	**Sixth Grade Can Really Kill You** Barthe DeClements	$2.75
❑ MT40409-1	**Sixth Grade Secrets** Louis Sachar	$2.75
❑ MT42882-9	**Sixth Grade Sleepover** Eve Bunting	$2.75
❑ MT41732-0	**Too Many Murphys** Colleen O'Shaughnessy McKenna	$2.75

Available wherever you buy books, or use this order form.

- -

Scholastic Inc., P.O. Box 7502, 2931 East McCarty Street, Jefferson City, MO 65102

Please send me the books I have checked above. I am enclosing $_____ (please add $2.00 to cover shipping and handling). Send check or money order — no cash or C.O.D.s please.

Name _____

Address _____

City_____ **State/Zip** _____

Please allow four to six weeks for delivery. Offer good in the U.S.A. only. Sorry, mail orders are not available to residents of Canada. Prices subject to change.

APP591

THE BABY-SITTERS CLUB®

by Ann M. Martin

The seven girls at Stoneybrook Middle School get into all kinds of adventures...with school, boys, and, of course, baby-sitting!

❑ NI43388-1	#1	**Kristy's Great Idea**	**$3.25**
❑ NI43513-2	#2	**Claudia and the Phantom Phone Calls**	**$3.25**
❑ NI43511-6	#3	**The Truth About Stacey**	**$3.25**
❑ NI43512-4	#4	**Mary Anne Saves the Day**	**$3.25**
❑ NI43720-8	#5	**Dawn and the Impossible Three**	**$3.25**
❑ NI43571-X	#48	**Jessi's Wish**	**$3.25**
❑ NI44970-2	#49	**Claudia and the Genius of Elm Street**	**$3.25**
❑ NI44969-9	#50	**Dawn's Big Date**	**$3.25**
❑ NI44968-0	#51	**Stacey's Ex-Best Friend**	**$3.25**
❑ NI44966-4	#52	**Mary Anne + 2 Many Babies**	**$3.25**
❑ NI44967-2	#53	**Kristy for President**	**$3.25**
❑ NI44965-6	#54	**Mallory and the Dream Horse**	**$3.25**
❑ NI44964-8	#55	**Jessi's Gold Medal**	**$3.25**
❑ NI45675-1	#56	**Keep Out, Claudia!**	**$3.25**
❑ NI45658-X	#57	**Dawn Saves the Planet**	**$3.25**
❑ NI44084-5		**Stacey and the Missing Ring Mystery #1**	**$3.25**
❑ NI44085-3		**Beware, Dawn! Mystery #2**	**$3.25**
❑ NI44799-8		**Mallory and the Ghost Cat Mystery #3**	**$3.25**
❑ NI44240-6		**Baby-sitters on Board! Super Special #1**	**$3.50**
❑ NI43576-0		**New York, New York! Super Special #6**	**$3.50**
❑ NI44963-X		**Snowbound Super Special #7**	**$3.50**
❑ NI44962-X		**Baby-sitters at Shadow Lake Super Special #8**	**$3.50**